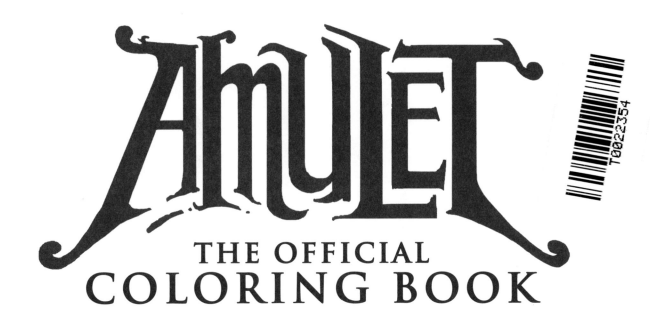

AMULET

THE OFFICIAL
COLORING BOOK

BASED ON THE BESTSELLING SERIES BY
KAZU KIBUISHI

graphix
AN IMPRINT OF
SCHOLASTIC

ISBN 978-1-339-01828-7

10 9 8 7 6 5 4 3 2 1   23 24 25 26 27

Printed in the U.S.A.   40
First printing 2023
Book design by Two Red Shoes Design

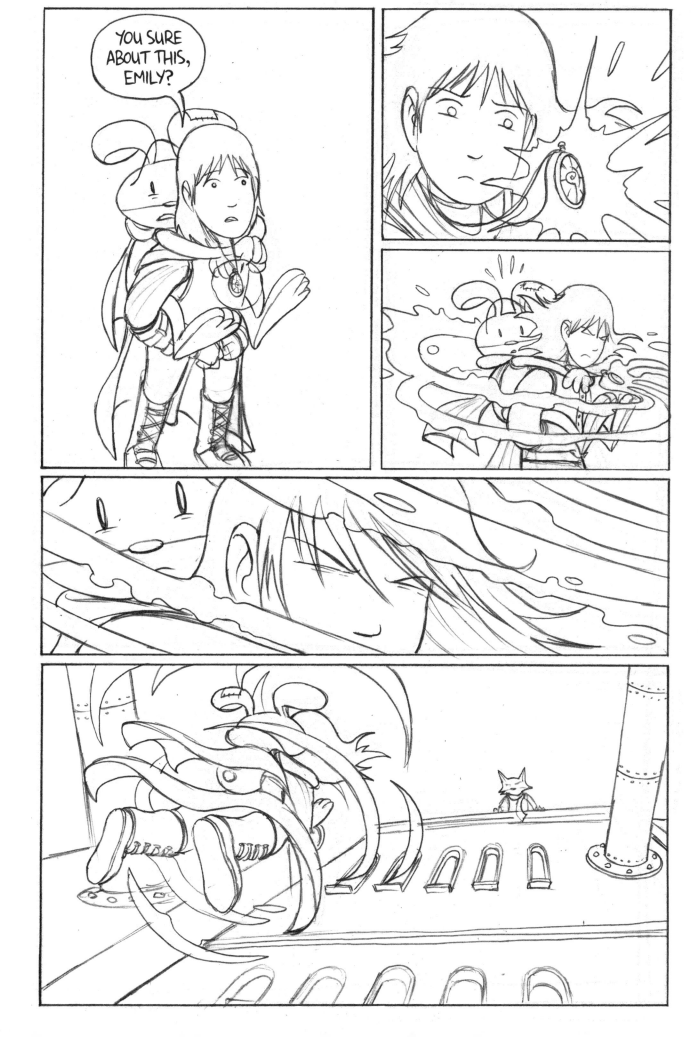

NAVIN HAYES
COMMANDER of the RESISTANCE

ALY HUNTER
PILOT

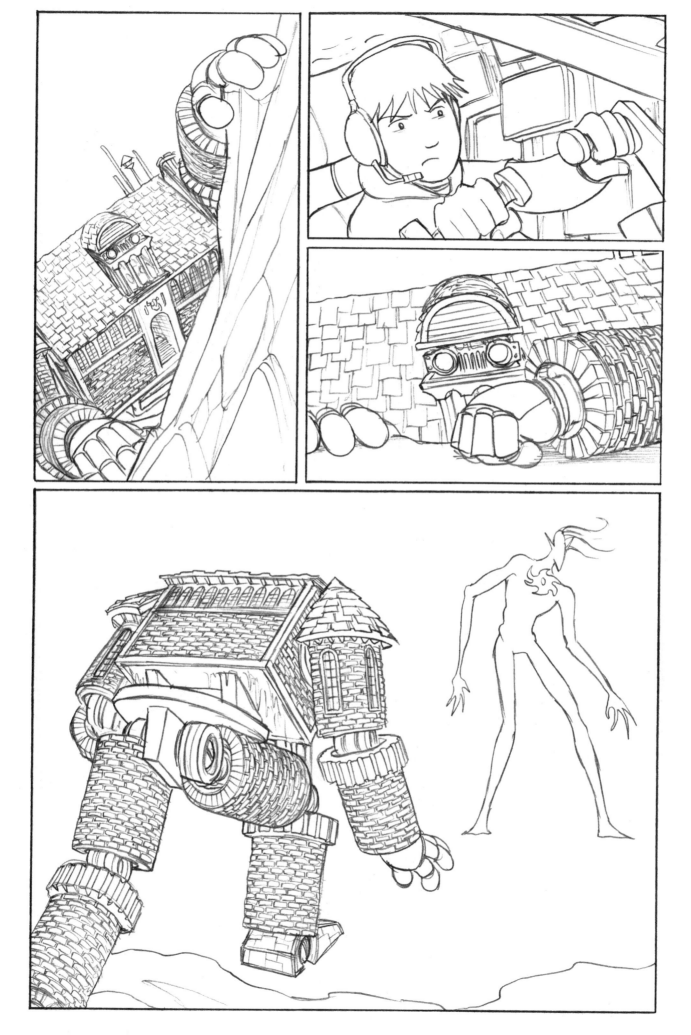

THE ELF KING

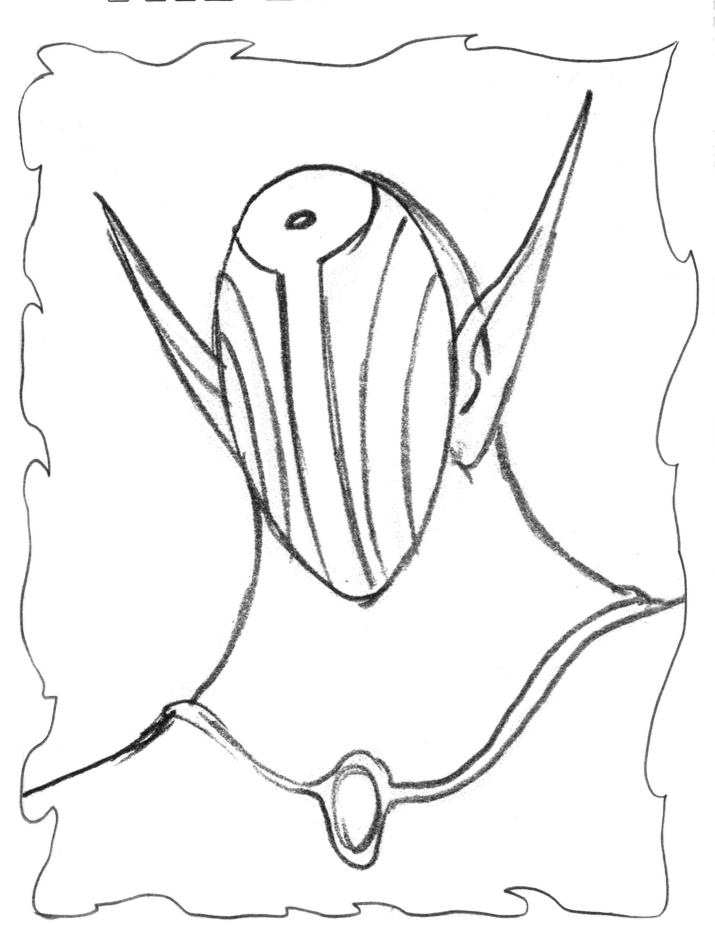

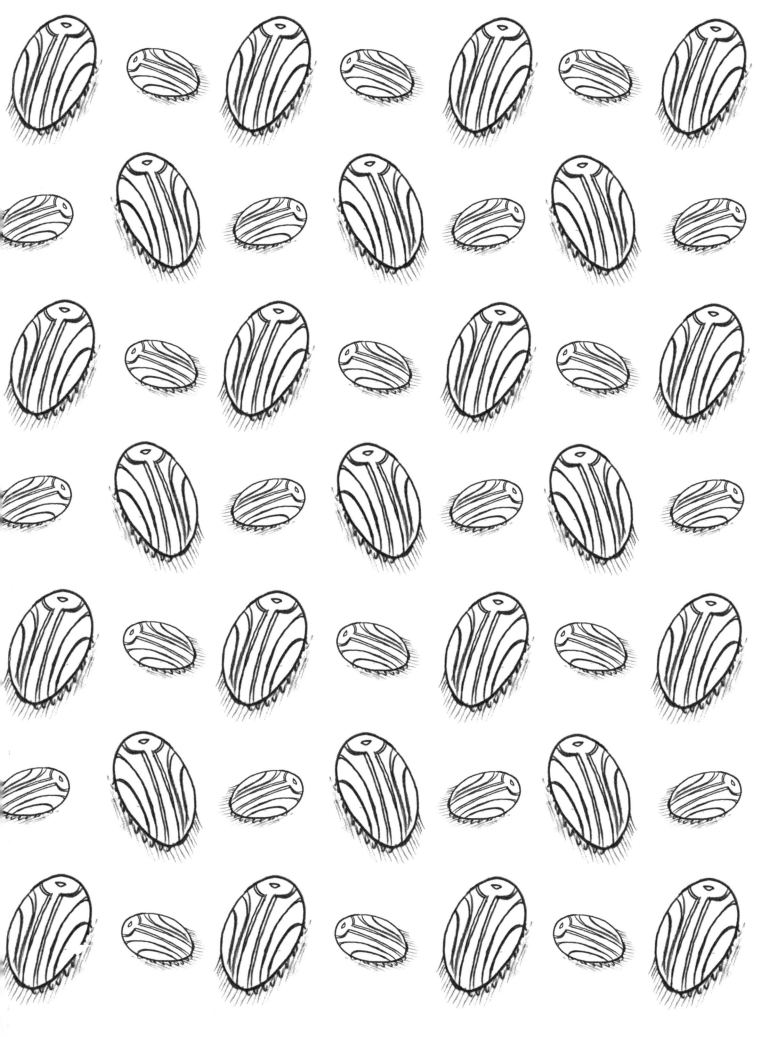

FREEING CHRONOS
FROM THE
ICE PRISON

MISKIT

LEON REDBEARD

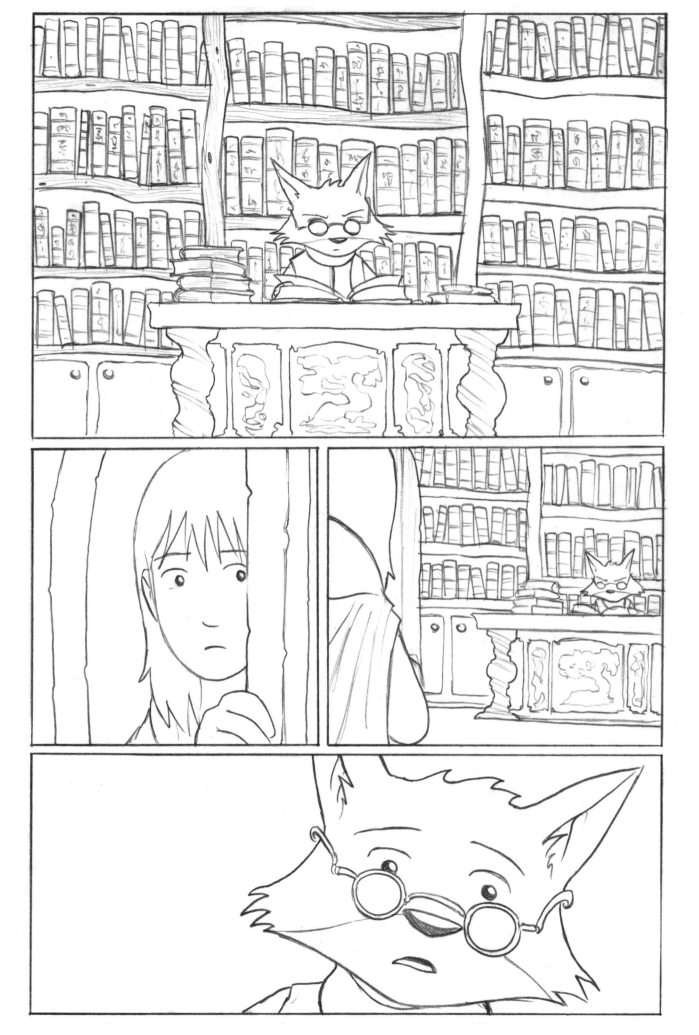

TRELLIS
SON OF THE ELF KING

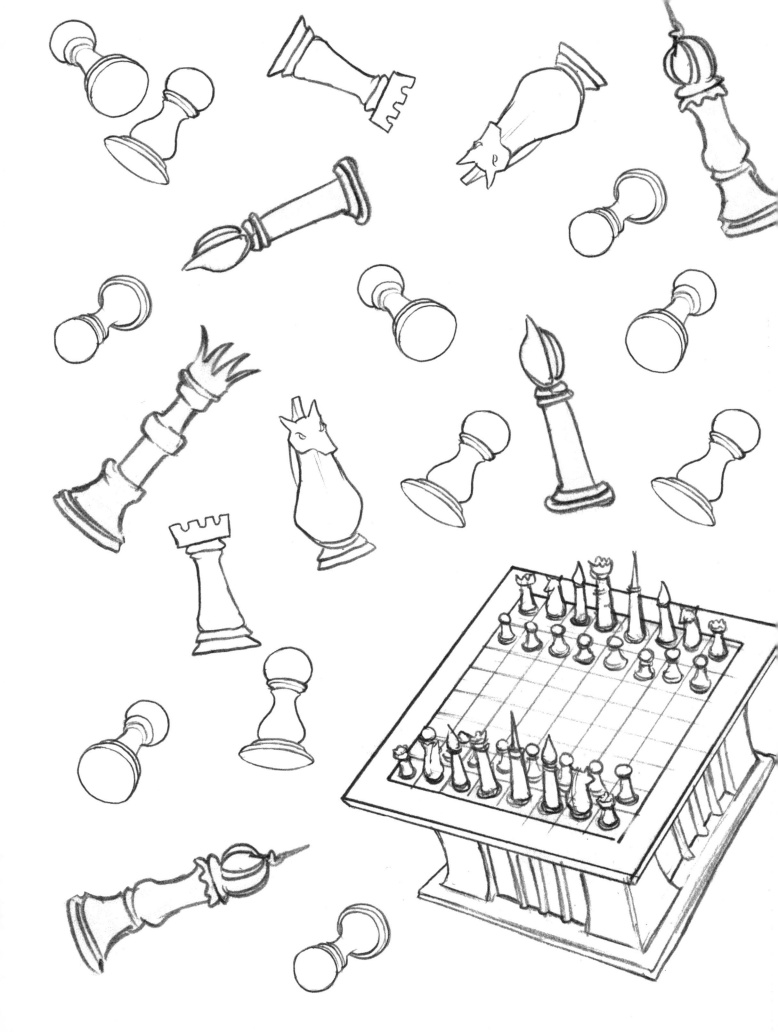

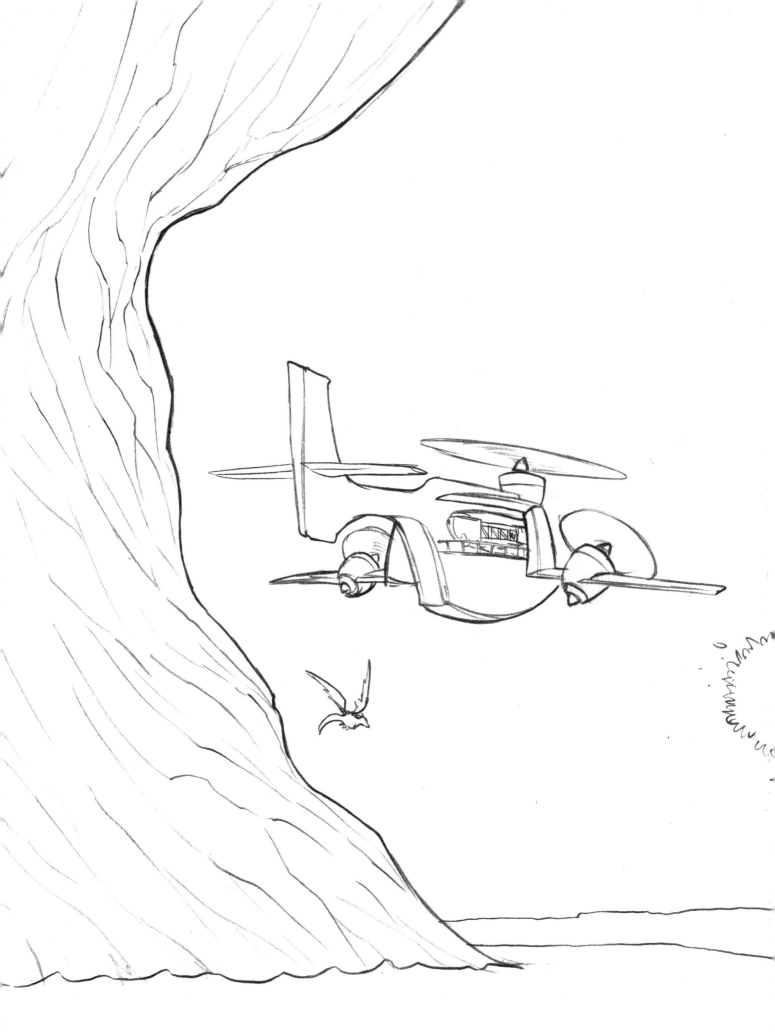

COGSLEY & DAGNO

ENZO & RICO
CREW OF THE *LUNA MOTH*

GABILAN

LOGI
SERVANT TO THE ELF KING

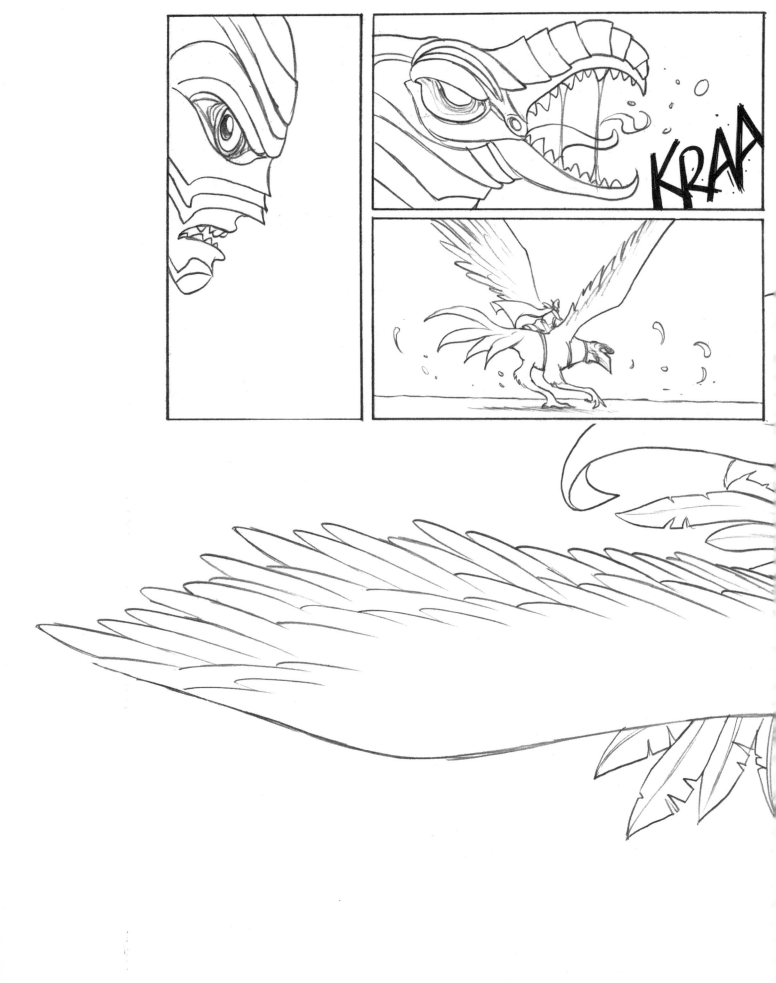

CHARNON HOUSE

VIGO LIGHT
STONEKEEPER

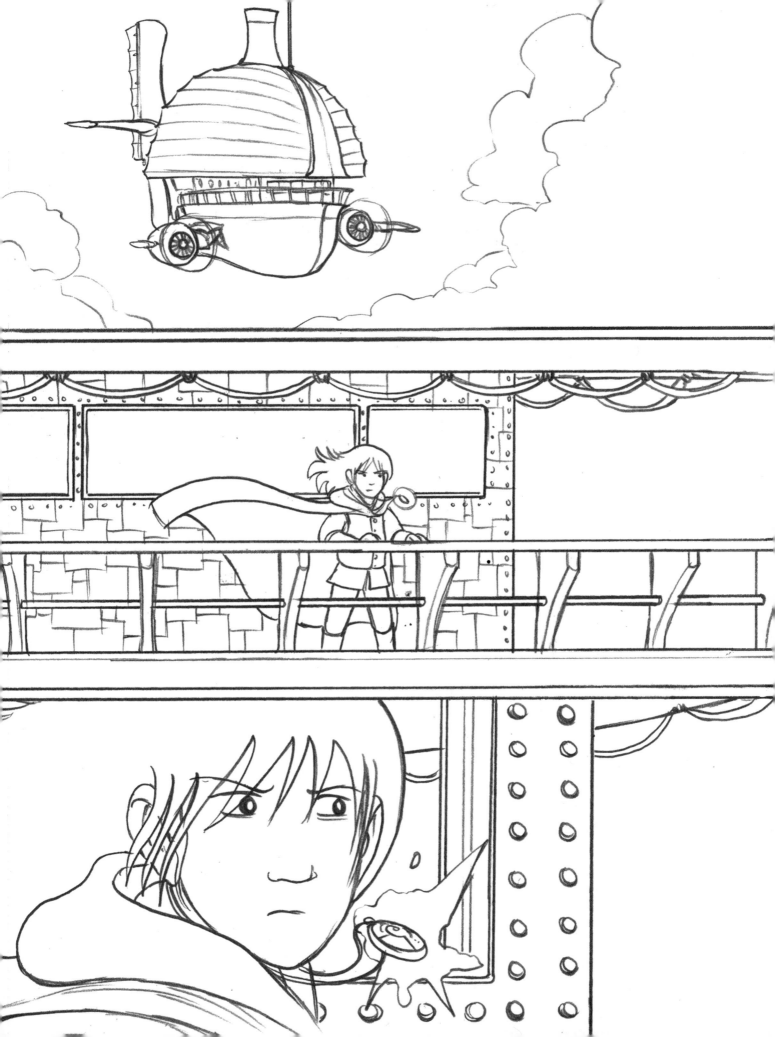

RIVA ASH
MAYOR OF LUCIEN

IKOL
THE VOICE OF
EMILY'S AMULET

MAX GRIFFIN
STONEKEEPER

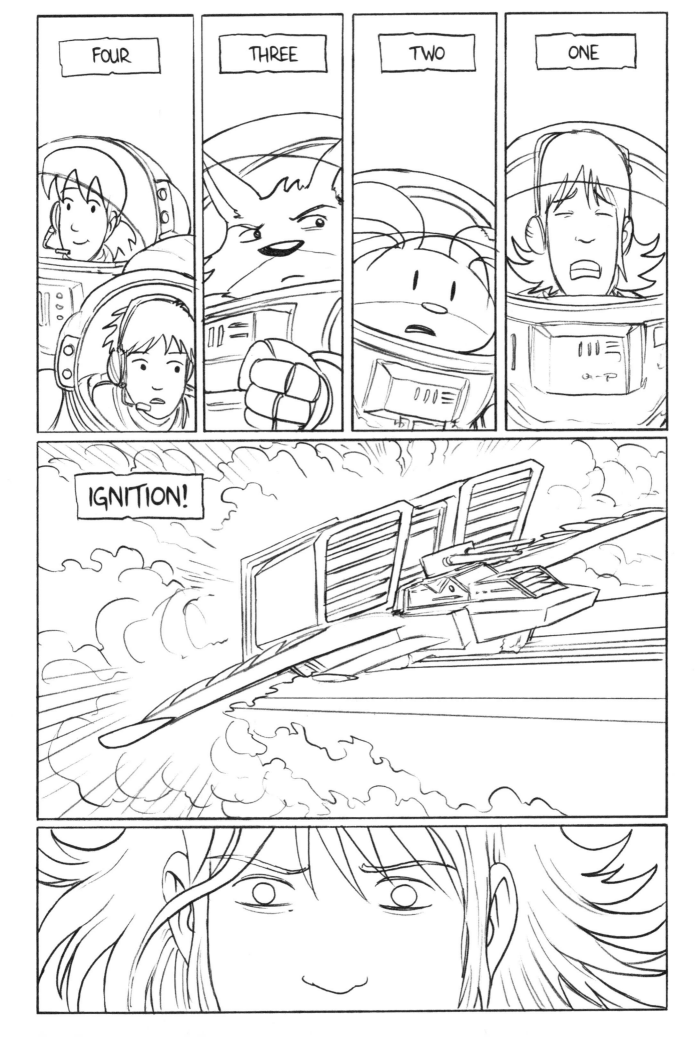